SONNY'S
TREASURE HUNT

To CHRIS,
my little treasure

Designed by Louise Millar
Printed and bound in Belgium by Proost
for the publishers, Piccadilly Press Ltd.,
5 Castle Road, London NW1 8PR

ISBNs: 1 85340 555 8 (hardback)
1 85340 571 X (paperback)

10 9 8 7 6 5 4 3 2 1

A catalogue record of this book is available from the British Library

Lisa Stubbs lives in Wakefield. She trained in Graphic Communications at Batley Art College and has illustrated greetings cards for a number of years. Her other books, SONNY'S WONDERFUL WELLIES, SONNY'S BIRTHDAY PRIZE and ED AND MR ELEPHANT: THE BIG SURPRISE are also published by Piccadilly Press:

SONNY'S BIRTHDAY PRIZE
ISBNs: 1 85340 422 5 (hardback)
1 85340 427 6 (paperback)

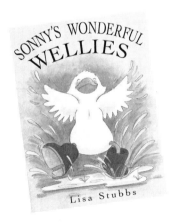

SONNY'S WONDERFUL WELLIES
ISBNs: 1 85340 369 5 (hardback)
1 85340 495 0 (paperback)

ED AND MR ELEPHANT
THE BIG SURPRISE
ISBNs: 1 85340 530 2 (hardback)
1 85340 565 5 (paperback)

SONNY'S
TREASURE HUNT

Piccadilly Press • London

Sonny was bored.

He had built houses with bricks.

He had looked at all his picture books,
and played for hours with his jumpy spider.

Sonny needed someone to play with.

"Mum, will you play with me?" shouted
Sonny over the noise of the vacuum cleaner.
"I'm busy," shouted Mum. "You can
always help me if you're bored."

"Will you play with me?" Sonny asked
Uncle Jim. "I'm bored."
"I'm too busy doing this weeding," said Uncle Jim.
"I wish I had the time to be bored."

Sonny phoned his friend Katie,
but she was going to visit her auntie.
"I'm bored out of my feathers," sighed Sonny
as he dragged his feet into the living-room
where Grandma was busy knitting.
"No one will play with me, Gran."

"When I was a young duckling and had no one
to play with," said Grandma, "my mum
would send me on a treasure hunt."
"Can I do one?" asked Sonny, looking excited.
"Yes!" cried Gran. "You stay here and I'll go
and hide the treasure. No peeking!"

When Grandma came back she handed
Sonny a piece of paper. "Here is a picture
of where the treasure is hidden."
The picture was of a teapot.
Sonny skipped into the kitchen.

Sonny looked in the cupboard.
He looked on the table.
He even looked under the table!

At last, he found the teapot by the sink.
Inside it was his first treasure and the next clue.

The picture was of a pair of red
wellies, and Sonny knew where
to find these.
"Wow!" said Sonny as he tipped
them upside-down and a ball
bounced onto the floor.
The next clue led Sonny up
to his own bed.

"What are you doing?" asked Mum
as Sonny looked under the bed.
"Looking for treasure," said Sonny.
"Can I help?" asked Mum as she started
searching the bed for treasure.
"Ah-ha!" cried Mum as she found a whistle
under Sonny's pillow.

The next clue was a watering can.
Mum and Sonny raced outside.
"*Stop!*" yelled Mum to Uncle Jim, who was
about to fill the watering can.

Mum explained the treasure hunt to Uncle Jim.
"What great fun," he said, as he pulled
a silly paper hat from the can. "Can I join in?
Let's see, the next clue is . . . the garden."

They looked behind the bushes.
They looked underneath the sunflowers.

They looked behind the trees.
Sonny was worried that everyone else
would find the treasure before he did.

Then Sonny yelled, "I've found it! I've found it!
I've found the treasure!"
He held up a huge bar of chocolate
and a bag of balloons. Everyone cheered.

Sonny had had a brilliant day, but he was tired.
"Tomorrow," said Sonny, with a beak full
of chocolate, "I think I'll play all by myself,
then I can be sure I find *all* the treasure!"